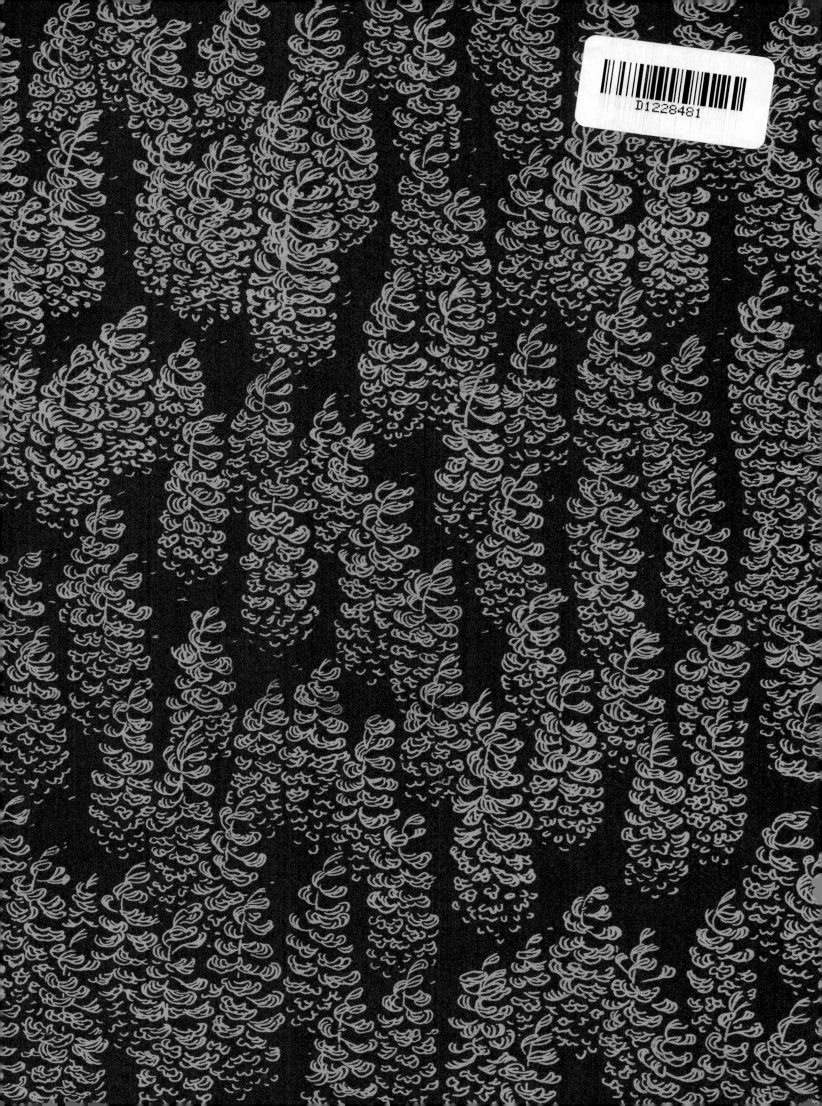

For every tree that has shared its story;
for all who have shared those stories;
and for all the storytellers to come

— T.S.

Published in English in 2021 by Owlkids Books Inc.
Originally published under the title *Quand le vent souffle*
Published with the permission of Comme des géants inc.,
38, rue Sainte-Anne, Varennes, Quebec, Canada, J3X 1R5
All rights reserved.
Translation rights arranged through the VeroK Agency, Barcelona, Spain

Owlkids Books acknowledges the financial support of the Canada Council for the
Arts, the Ontario Arts Council, the Government of Canada through the Canada
Book Fund (CBF), and the Government of Ontario through the Ontario Creates
Book Initiative for our publishing activities.

Published in Canada by
Owlkids Books Inc.
1 Eglinton Avenue East
Toronto, ON M4P 3A1

Published in the United States by
Owlkids Books Inc.
1700 Fourth Street
Berkeley, CA 94710

Library and Archives Canada Cataloguing in Publication

Title: The wind and the trees / Todd Stewart.
Names: Stewart, Todd (Illustrator), author.
Identifiers: Canadiana 20200259296 | ISBN 9781771474337 (hardcover)
Classification: LCC PS8637.T497 W56 2019 | DDC jC813/.6—dc23

Library of Congress Control Number: 2020939450

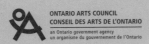
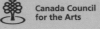

Manufactured in Guangdong Province, Dongguan City, China, in October 2020
by Toppan Leefung Packaging & Printing (Dongguan) Co., Ltd.
Job #BAYDC80

A   B   C   D   E   F

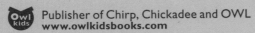

Publisher of Chirp, Chickadee and OWL
www.owlkidsbooks.com

Owlkids Books is a division of bayard canada

Todd Stewart

the Wind and the Trees

Owlkids Books

Hello!

Hello.

What a windy day!

You'll get used to it, little one.

Up here, the wind always blows,
day and night, year after year.

I like the wind.

It feels good.

The wind can hurt too.

Although the soil is rich, and I get plenty of
sunshine and just enough rain . . .

... the blowing wind pulls and shapes me.
It stretches my roots, dries me out,
and will break me apart.

Then I don't like the wind!

The wind also helps me.
It scatters my seeds so new trees
can grow where others have fallen.

As the wind blows against me,
my roots grow deeper and my
bark becomes stronger.

The wind carries my messages
and signals to other trees in the forest.
And it lets us talk to each other!

So how do you feel about the wind?

I embrace it. Like this!

I want to try!

I feel a storm coming.
Let's embrace the wind together!

Okay, I'm ready!

It scatters my seeds …

*It makes my roots
grow deeper …*

It carries my messages …

Hello, little one.

Oh! Hello!

The End